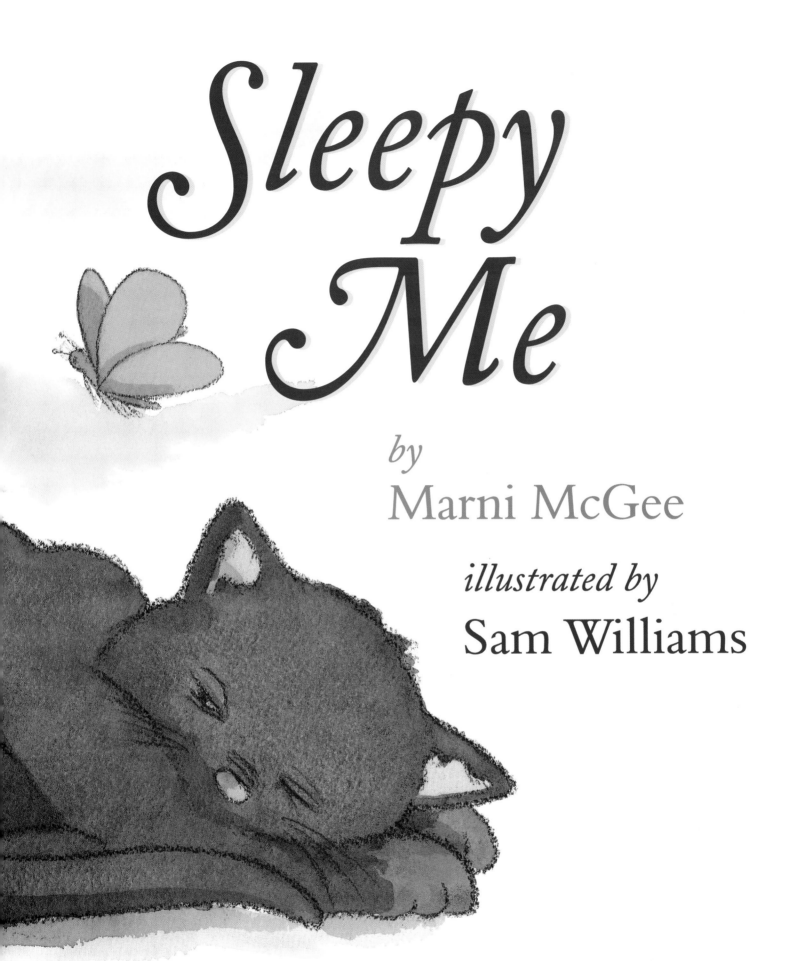

Sleepy Me

by

Marni McGee

illustrated by

Sam Williams

SIMON & SCHUSTER BOOKS FOR YOUNG READERS
NEW YORK   LONDON   TORONTO   SYDNEY   SINGAPORE

 SIMON & SCHUSTER BOOKS FOR YOUNG READERS
An imprint of Simon & Schuster Children's Publishing Division
1230 Avenue of the Americas, New York, New York 10020
Text copyright © 2001 by Marni McGee
Illustrations copyright © 2001 by Sam Williams
All rights reserved including the right of reproduction in whole or in part in any form.
SIMON & SCHUSTER BOOKS FOR YOUNG READERS is a trademark of Simon & Schuster.
Book design by Joyce White
The text for this book is set in Aldine.
The illustrations are rendered in watercolor.
Printed in Hong Kong
10 9 8 7 6 5 4 3 2 1
Library of Congress Cataloging-in-Publication Data
McGee, Marni.
Sleepy me / by Marni McGee ; illustrated by Sam Williams.—1st ed.
    p. cm.
Summary: As everything in the house winds down, Daddy carries a sleepy child to bed.
ISBN 0-689-82378-9
[1. Bedtime—Fiction. 2. Father and child—Fiction. 3. Stories in rhyme.] I. Williams, Sam,
ill. II. Title.   PZ8.3.M4595458S1 2000   [E]—dc21   98-19971   CIP   AC

In loving memory of Claude U. Broach—preacher and poet, lover of life, singer of songs . . . writer, father, friend
—M. M.

For Brenda, Richard, and Becky
—S. W.

Sleepy cat.

Sleepy mouse.

Sleepy sounds
inside the house.

Sleepy stair.

Sleepy chair.

Sleepy Daddy

rocks me there.

Sleepy bookcase.

Sleepy ball.

Sleepy mirror sees it all.

Sleepy star.
Sleepy tree.

Sleepy breeze blows in on me.

Sleepy story.
Sleepy sighs.

Sleepy Mom
will kiss my eyes.

Sleepy bed
with *sleepy*
bear.

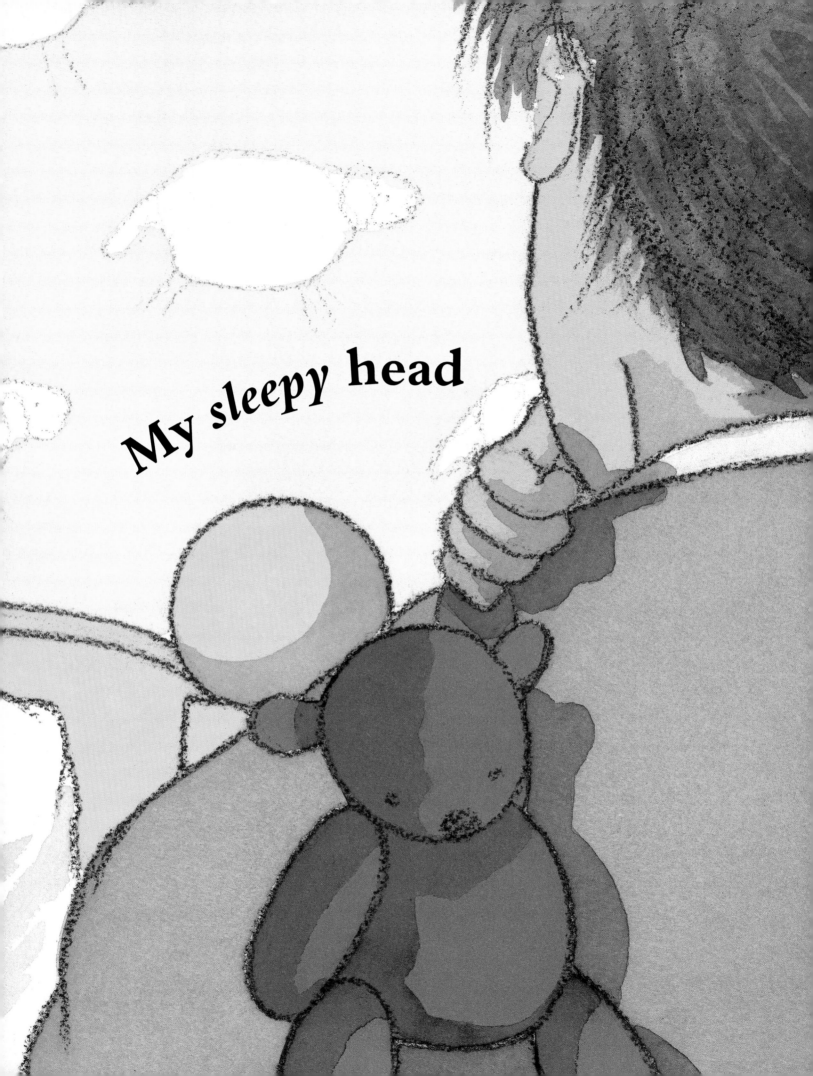

My sleepy head

will soon be there.

Sleepy me,
sleeping tight.
Sleeping till the
morning light.